D1487674

My

The Ratchet Conclusion

No Place Like Home

I came to a screeching halt in my parent's driveway. I knew it was only going to be a matter of time before the police tracked me there so I had to move quickly. Not only was I exhausted from driving almost 12 hours, I was starving and didn't want to take any chances stopping off on the road. Plus I was still reeling over the fact that I had to kill the man I loved. I didn't want it to come to that but I had no choice.

Even though I had successfully made it over the state line and into Tennessee, I still needed to be extra careful. Not only did I need to grab a quick shower; this would be an opportunity for AJ to meet his grandparents for the first time. Not to mention the fact that they hadn't seen me in almost six years.

Momma knew I was a woman because I had confessed it to her during one of my break downs. But as far as I knew she still hadn't told daddy. That didn't make me one bit of difference. This was going to possibly be the first and last time he had seen his oldest son in years. He could chose to accept me for who I had become, or risk losing me and AJ from his life altogether.

"Lemme in!" I yelled as I banged on the door. I was a nervous wreck, if momma didn't open this door quick, fast, and in a hurry I would have to kick it in.

"Who is it?" my daddy barked from the other side of the door.

"Daddy it's me Peyton, open the door," I replied as I frantically jerked on the knob.

"Go away from here! I don't have a son!" he protested.

"Peyton is that you?" Momma asked as she yanked the door open.

"My God son, is that really you?" She asked.

My mother and father stood in the middle of the living room floor staring at me like they had seen a ghost. I sat AJ's carrier down on the sofa and pulled my mom into my arms.

"It's really me momma," I wept. "And this is your grandson AJ."

After holding me and crying for what seemed like an eternity, she then turned her attention to AJ; she cradled him and covered him in kisses before placing him back into his seat.

"He so handsome Peyton," she announced through a veil of tears.

"What the hell Vivian? I can't believe you let this monster up in here!" my father hissed.

"Frank! This is your son! Can we at least try and hear him out?" my mother pleaded.

"That's no son of mine. I haven't seen my son since he graduated from high school," he fumed. "Humph! Had everybody worried sick about his ass for years, now he shows up, on the run looking like some kind of damn circus freak."

My father's eyebrows were in a knot and the vein on his neck was pulsating. It was obvious he was infuriated.

"Frank! Please!" she yelled.

"Naw, its ok momma, let him speak his mind."

"Please my ass Vivian! This nigga standing here with titties bigger than yours, I don't know how you even have the nerve to come back here after all the worry you have cause us. Do you know how many nights your momma done stayed up crying, praying you were ok? And you didn't even have the decency to pay us a visit since you left. But soon as your ass gets in trouble you remember where home is."

"Peyton he didn't mean that," momma insisted.

"I told you, its ok momma, I deserve every bit of that." I stood silently weeping as my father called me every inhumane name under the sun. His fury knew no boundaries. And when it was all said and done I couldn't exactly blame him. His first born son had not only transformed into his daughter without his knowledge; I was also on the run for murder. It was a lot for anyone to take in, especially an elderly man set in his ways such as my father.

"Peyton...,"my mother called out to me.

"Please momma, call me Pebbles."

"I'm sorry... Pebbles," she responded as the tears flooded her eyes. We saw you on **Hoodz Most Wanted**. Please tell me that you didn't do all those horrible things they are saying about you. I know we raised you better than that. Please tell me you didn't kill those girls."

It tore me apart to see my momma hurting like this. In a perfect world this all would have been a bad dream and when we woke up everything would be beautiful. Adrian and I would still be together, Tasha would still be alive and my parents would be enjoying their new grandson. But this was real life and my nightmare had just begun. I wanted desperately to lie to my mother and tell her that the accusations were false but the words just wouldn't escape my lips. I wanted to promise her everything was going to be ok but the truth was, I had no idea where my life was headed from here on out. In the past lying came with ease, but since all my ratchet secrets were on display for the world to see there was no reason to hide.

"I did what I had to do for love momma," I whispered through the tears.

"This is some bullshit if I've even seen it!" my father barked. "Of course he did it He's a damn demon. He killed Tasha and that surrogate and God knows what to Adrian. You getting yo' crazy ass up out of here."

My mother began shaking uncontrollably. My confession had come as such a shock to her that she actually fell into a chair to keep from passing out, "Oh God! Please tell me you didn't kill Adrian too."

"I tried to love him momma but he refused to love me back once he found out who I really was. I sacrificed my whole life for that man, only to have him throw me away like I was nothing. I had to do it momma."

"That's it! I've heard enough," My daddy announced as he headed for the telephone. "I knew that shit was true when I saw your sick ass up on that TV screen. I tried to call Adrian and warn him but I guess I was too late. Damn! Where the hell did I go wrong raising you?" He shook his head in disbelief. "I'm calling the police."

"Put that damn phone down!" Peyton yelled as he pushed my father to the ground and knocked the phone from his hand.

"Pebbles! Stop it!" my mother begged. "Please just leave the baby with us to raise and turn yourself in."

"That wasn't me momma, that was Peyton, he takes over my body sometimes," I replied, speaking in my normal feminine voice.

"I told you, he's damn freak! Get the hell out of here and take that damn test tube baby with you!" my father blurted out. As he tried to get up off the floor Peyton knocked him flat of his back before placing a foot on his neck.

"Slow ya' roll old man before you end up like Adrian," Peyton replied.

My parents were terrified as they watched me switch between Pebbles and Peyton with ease. It had been a long time since he had emerged but the stressful situation triggered a relapse.

"What's the matter daddy, you don't love your daughter?" Peyton asked.

My father began gripping his chest and wincing in pain.

"Daddy! I'm sorry!" Peyton cried out. "UGH!! UGH!! I didn't mean to hurt you and momma, but I can't go to jail." I flat out did the ugly cry in Peyton's voice as I took the pressure off of his neck. Before I could say another word my mother had run over to come to his assistance.

"Frank! Are you ok?" she asked as she pushed me out of the way. "Is it your heart?"

He nodded as he gasped for air.

"Look at what you have done!" She screamed before pulling a cell phone from out of her apron pocket.

By now AJ was awake and crying. My body wanted to react from my father's distress. Lord knows I hoped I hadn't given him a heart attack. But it was like I was frozen in time. I was snapped back into reality by my mother's voice.

"911 emergency? Yes get here quick, I believe my husband is having a heart attack."

Oh shit! She just called 911. I had to make a move, and fast!

"Just relax sweetheart help is on the way," she consoled him before turning her attention back to me.

"Lord knows we done tried to raise you the best we knew how. And we done tried to do right by you. But I'll be damned if I'm gonna let you bring those wicked ways up in this house and hurt me or your father. You have made your bed, now lie in it. You can do what's right and turn yourself in. Or you can continue to run like you've been doing, the choice is yours. Either way I've washed my hands to you. The paramedics are on the way and I'm sure the police won't be far behind so you better make your mind up quick.

My mother's voice was stern as she stared me dead in my eyes. It was like she had changed into a different person. All the sweetness and softness had gone out the window when she felt like my father's life was in danger. It was like I was a little kid all over again. I choked on my tears as I bundled up AJ and prepared to take off. This could possibly be the last time I saw my parents. Once my sis and little bro found out what I had done they cut me off years ago. I had now lost momma in my corner as well.

I quickly kissed my momma and told my father I was sorry once again before telling him that I loved him. He didn't bother to respond. His eyes were glazed as he looked off into the distance. When it was all said and done I fled from my parent's home, taking my son with me. I promised momma that I would try to call and see how daddy was doing, but she told me not to bother. I had let her down for the final time.

Man Vs Wild

Where the fuck am I? Adrian thought as he gazed around in the pitch blackness. The last thing he remembered was Pebbles beating him with a two by four.

Each attempt to move on his part was met with excruciating pain. Not only had he been shot in the knee, his leg was broken and twisted from the fall he had taken when she dumped him over the edge of the cliff. His head was throbbing and he seemed to only have use of one of his eyes. The other one was only able to pick up shadows. His shoulder also felt like it had been dislocated, and several of his ribs felt like they were shattered.

Glancing down, he noticed his blood stained clothing glistening in the moonlight. It wasn't until he tried to move his hand to his head to investigate his wounds did he realize that his wrists were still bound with the duct tape.

"Shit!" He yelp in agony as he tried to scoot himself in an upright position.

His broadcast was met with a reply of a low throaty growl. Something was in his presence. And judging by the cracking of leaves caused by footsteps it seemed to be moving closer.

Adrian was petrified to say the least. Not only had he been beaten and left for dead in the wilderness, it was dark and he was bound with no way of protecting himself. Because he had been knocked unconscious for quite a while, he had no sense of time. He did however, have enough sense to understand that he was in danger. It was obvious that some kind of wild animal was lurking nearby.

The kind of animal would soon be revealed as Adrian cried out in pain when he tried to move. He soon heard the howling of a lone coyote. At this point he realized that it was imperative that he break free if he was going to have any chance at survival.

After dragging himself to a nearby tree and propping himself up, he then felt around for anything that he could use to cut himself free. Once he secured a small stone in his grasp he used the sharp edge to saw away at the thick tape. This proved to be a daunting task seeing as his hands were behind his back.

As he grunted and sawed away he soon realized that he was no longer alone. He held his breath and turned his head to listen for any sounds other than crickets singing and branches swaying in the wind. His body was swept with sheer terror as he listened to the slow pant that sounded like it was right in front of him. His heart sank to his stomach as he focused on the two beady eyes that flashed in the darkness. The coyote was standing right beside him!

"Get out of here!" he yelled as he frantically twisted his wrists trying to break free.

The beast answered with a howl that sent chills down Adrian's spine. Apparently it was dinner time and he was the main course. And the aroma of fresh blood made him all the more appetizing. The fact that he was possibly about to be attacked didn't frighten him as much as what would come next. The more he proceeded to yell at the animal to try and scare it away; its howls became louder and more progressive, finally being met by other howls in the distance.

"What the fuck! He calling his boys, I gotta get the hell out of here!"

Suddenly, the animal turned its attention to something else. Adrian had no idea what piqued the animal's interest but he prayed that it would be enough to give him the break he needed to escape. As luck would have it the coyote ran off to chase the smaller prey he'd locked his focus on.

Now's my chance, he thought. He didn't know how long he had before the animal would return, but one thing was for certain, he didn't want to be there when it did.

After what seemed like an eternity of rubbing his wrists against the stone he finally severed the tape. Exhausted, frightened, and bleeding now from his wrists as well he was able to crawl out of the open and into the shelter of a large bush. He buried himself in the leaves and lay there weeping, praying for daylight.

When daybreak finally arrived he was awakened by a tickling sensation. He opened his eyes to see his entire body covered in carpenter ants.

"What the fuck!" he screamed as his body thrashed about on the ground. After brushing off as many ants as he could he then made his way to the chilly lake, walked in and completely submerged himself.

"Shit shit shit!!!," he yelled as his body clenched up from the frigid temperature.

Even though the water was a bone chilling 45 degrees it had its benefits. Not only did it cleanse his open wounds, it further slowed down the bleeding on his knee. However it wasn't long before Adrian realized that he'd better make his way back to shore as quickly as possible to avoid hyperthermia.

As he sat on the ground shivering uncontrollably it suddenly hit him, if Pebbles had in fact left the scene she would have done so in the getaway car that she had stowed away there. This would have meant that their vehicle would still be there. All he needed to do was make his way back up the hill. This would prove to be easier said than done. By now he was weak from hunger and blood loss, as well as his body was too broken up to make the journey. The only saving grace he got from the cold was the fact that his body was actually becoming numb to the pain. One thing that was for certain, if he stayed there he faced an uncertain death.

Adrian would spend the next two days trying to make his way back up the hill. At this point he had totally given up on trying to find the car. Not only was he completely lost; he was fading in and out of consciousness. The only thing that kept him alive and moving was pure adrenalin and the sheer will to live. After he finally managed to pull himself up the last few feet of the muddy slope he drug his near lifeless body to the edge of the road where he would pass out for good.

He would be found later that day by a lone traveler who called for help.

Road To Recovery

"Mr. Ramsey? Can you hear me?"

Adrian blinked and tried to focus on the figure that stood over him. No sooner than he opened his eyes a beam of light flashed on his pupils causing him to squint.

"Mr. Ramsey I'm Dr Youvall. You are in County Medical Hospital. Do you understand?"

Adrian nodded his head.

"Are you able to speak?" the Dr. asked.

"Yes," he replied in a low whisper.

"Good, now can you tell me who the president of the United States is?"

"Obama?"

"Very good, you were brought in with life threating injuries, including a concussion. I'm going to step out and grab your x-rays and your chart. When I return I will go over the nature of your injuries and suggested treatment. Meanwhile you have some visitors waiting for you," he replied before stepping out of the room.

Adrian couldn't quite remember what had happened to him. All he knew was that his body felt like it had been hit by a semi-truck. He felt extremely tired and disoriented. From his room he could hear bickering in the hallway.

"So he's awake? That means we can go in for questioning?" the officer asked the doctor.

"I'm afraid not," he replied.

"Absolutely not!" Adrian's mother protested. She had been by his side the entire time he was unconscious. Her child had been through hell already. There was no way she was going to let the cops badger him as soon as he opened his eyes.

"Mrs. Ramsey we understand that you are upset but the sooner he's coherent enough to give us a description of who did this to him, the faster we can catch them," another cop chimed in.

"We already know who did this to him! It was that maniac Pebbles! You should be out there looking for her instead of here trying to harass my son," she yelled.

"With all due respect ma'am we are doing everything in our power to track her down. But we also can't be certain if it was her until your son gives us a statement. And if it is her we need to know if she was working alone. Rest assured that there will be an officer standing guard in case anyone other than a doctor or a nurse tries to enter the room."

"Mrs. Ramsey you may go in and see him now," the doctor announced, seeing that she was visibly upset. He would try to hold the officers off from questioning him for as long as possible, till he was certain his patient was up to it.

Upon entering the room Adrian's mother broke down into tears. She had already buried one child at the hands of Pebbles and she almost lost another. Her heart was heavy with sadness over the death of Tasha, but at the same time she was over joyed to see her baby boy awake and talking. Once his father was done drilling the officers about his son's protection he joined her in the room as well.

This was the beginning of a long and treacherous journey for Adrian, between the visits from family and friends, to the constant questioning from the FBI. He felt like his whole world had been turned upside down. His statement, along with the evidence at the scene of the crime in the woods put them one step closer to finding Pebbles. Until then there was nothing else to do but wait.

Dr Lean

"I wish you would stop all that noise," the nurse teased. The slow tapping of Adrian's fingers on his cast was driving her insane.

"Huh? Oh my bad," Adrian replied in a half sleep state. He had finally made it home from the hospital, however the injuries he sustained were major; a concussion, ruptured eye socket, three cracked ribs, a fractured shoulder, a shattered femur due to the gunshot wound on his left knee, and several contusions across his body. Not only did he still have a cast on his leg, he was having migraines and still hadn't regained full use of his right eye. He had to have a visiting nurse five days a week. His mom took over on the weekends.

The duration of his recovery time so far had been a combination of sleep, being hopped up on pain medication, and grueling physical therapy. As a matter of fact he'd been so out of it that he still hadn't fully wrapped his brain around what had happened to him. At this point he was still in a state of shock and denial. Not to mention the fact that since his concussion his memory dipped in and out. What he could remember played out like a nightmare that he tried hard to forget. He figured if he pushed the painful memories to the back of his mind it was like they didn't exist. The only reality for him was the dreaded memory of his son AJ. He was out there someone with that lunatic Pebbles. He made a vow to himself just as he did when his sister Tasha was killed; he wouldn't rest until her killer was caught and brought to justice. In this case Pebbles was both a murderer and a kidnapper.

So far the only lead he had was a card he found of the doctor she was seeing when she pretended to have eggs extracted. The very thought of how many lies were fed to him made almost as sick to the stomach as knowing his wife, the love of his life was really a man.

This muthafucka' was Pebbles' primary physician. He sat right up in Adrian's face and lied about the procedure, as well as what he was treating her for. He had to be in on the plot. The only question was why. What the hell was he getting out of the deal? Who knows, maybe he and Pebbles were running the scam together the whole time. In any case all he needed was proof, and that's what exactly what he intended to get. By now he was certain that the FBI had exhausted all efforts in question the Doc. Still, that didn't stop Adrian. He knew that quack had something to do with his son's disappearance and he was determined to prove it one way or another.

When the nurse stepped out for a break he made his call.

"Dr Johnson's office, how may I direct your call?" the receptionist asked.

"Yes, is the doctor available?" Adrian asked.

"He's just finishing up with a patient. Would you like to hold? It may be a few moments."

"Yes I'll wait."

"Great! Who shall I say is calling?"

"Tell him it's Pebbles."

What the hell does she want? I thought I was finally done with this crazy bitch? Why is she still stalking me? The Doc thought. *She got some fucking nerve after that shit she pulled at the convention. Got the police all up on my ass, I don't need this shit. I gotta get rid of this hoe once and for all.*

After instructing the receptionist to hold all calls and appointments he reluctantly picked up the phone.

"Listen here Pebbles we don't have any business! Don't contact me here again!" The Doc shouted.

"Where should I contact you at then?" Adrian asked.

"What? Who is this?" The Doc asked nervously, now realizing that his anger may have caused him to speak to soon.

"It's Adrian, Pebbles' husband."

What the fuck is he contacting me for?" The Doc thought. *"I don't need any more unneeded heat. I done already told the police I don't know shit.*

For a split second he thought about hanging up the phone but he figured that it would be best to play it cool.

"Ahem… yes Mr. Ramsey, how may I help you?"

"You sure picked up the phone with the quickness when you thought it was Pebbles. What the hell kind of damn scam are you two running? And where the hell is my son?" Adrian fumed.

"Now just a minute, I don't know what you are talking about," The Doc replied defensibly.

"Bullshit! You were in on every lie Pebbles told about not being able to have children, extracting eggs, and the real egg donor, hell you knew she was man the whole time and didn't say shit. Did that surrogate Fallyn come from your office? You know she's dead right? Did you know that Pebbles killed her? Did you know that she tried to kill me?"

Adrian hurled the questions and accusations at The Doc with lightning speed. He was determined to get to the truth or at least trip him up in a lie. Little to his knowledge, despite The Doc being nervous, he was prepared to answer anything that was asked of him.

"Slow down, I don't know anything about your son missing. I told the same thing to the police. I have given them my full cooperation. Pebbles and I are not in any kind of scheme together," he responded confidently. He'd already skated past prison from his encounter with **Club Double Cup**, he wasn't about to let this young punk assed nigga catch him up.

"Then why lie nigga? Why the hell didn't you say anything about that muthafucka being a man when I was in your office?"

"Patient/ doctor confidentiality agreement, I'm not required to share that information. Besides, how would I know you didn't know? I'm not up in y'all's bedroom. I mean that's a shame what happened to those girls, but as I stated before. I don't know anything."

"Those girls have a name. One is Tasha, my sister, the other is Fallyn. She killed them both. There is a cold blooded killer on the loose with my son and you holding out on information. Did you tell the police about the surrogate and donor? Did you tell them that you lied to a patient's husband about the procedures being performed? Even if you couldn't share the information about her being a man, that was still some foul shit that went down. How do you sleep at night?" Adrian asked.

This nigga really thought he had something on the Doc. Little did he know that soon as Fallyn came up dead Dr Johnson destroyed all files from Pebbles, Fallyn, and the donor. He knew it was only going to be a matter of time before the FBI came knocking and he made sure they didn't find shit. At this point it was Adrian's word against his. However, despite how everything went down he did actually feel remorse about what happened to Fallyn, seeing as he helped give Pebbles the tools she needed to kill her. It was a mistake he would have to live with for the rest of his life and he prayed for forgiveness every night. He felt bad for Adrian also. He realized that he was a desperate man, grasping for anything he could find out about his son. For that reason he decided that he would at least come halfway straight with him.

"I knew she used to be a man but I didn't feel the need to pass the word. Hell I figured you were her husband, you should have already known. How the hell was I supposed to know she was lying to your ass?"

"The fact that you were lying for her about having endometriosis and not being able to have kids! That's how!" Adrian snapped. *Is this bastard even listening to himself?*

Touché my nigga, the Doc thought. "Look imma keep it 100. I went along with the lie about Pebbles not being able to get pregnant cause I was getting paid, plain and simple. A nigga trying to get his hustle on just like everybody else, I didn't know anything would become of it. And I will admit I did have feelings for Mittens but she was in love with you."

"Who the fuck is Mittens?"

"That was my nickname for Pebbles; once upon a time she had the sexiest man hands I had ever laid eyes on. I had a crush on her but that's as far as it went, I swear."

Adrian sighed, as much as he hated to admit it The Doc actually sounded like he was telling the truth. There was no question that he was a weirdo his damn self and he could have gone on taking shots at his character all day long, but that still wouldn't make him know anything, or tell it if he did. And it certainly wasn't going to bring his son back. At the end of the day he was just a simple minded asshole that was out for a dollar and for all he knew Pebbles could have threatened him as well. The best he could hope for was to try and stay on The Doc's good side in case she tried to contact him.

"Either you don't know shit, or you ain't saying shit," Adrian hissed. "Whatever the case may be, I need you to call me immediately if she contacts you. I'll make it worth your while. When was the last time you heard from her?" he asked.

When that crazy muthafucka crashed my convention, attacked my woman and ran off with my shit! The Doc thought, but he couldn't say any of this to Adrian. Nor could he tell him that Pebbles contacted him before she fled town.

"I haven't seen or heard from her since she last visited the office with you," he replied.

Sensing that he wasn't going to get any more information out of the Doc. Adrian decided to cut the conversation short.

"Alright well like I said; contact me if you hear from her."

"Will do," The Doc responded before hanging up the phone in relief. He had skated past trouble once again.

Life On The Run

"What the hell are you staring at?" I asked the cashier at the 711 as she rang up my order. I normally didn't make junk food runs in the day time but a bitch was fiending for some Krispy Kreams and I needed to get some milk for AJ.

Instead of responding she leaned towards her coworker who was standing nearby and mumbled something under her breath. I don't what they were saying but I knew it was about me and I didn't like it one bit. At any given moment my ass could be recognized so I had to play it cool and get the hell out of there. This was my first time venturing out in months for fear of being caught.

Even though momma said she had washed her hands to me she still let me leave without turning me in. I know for a fact if daddy had that chance he would have my ass locked far away in someone's jail cell with the key thrown away. And I can't say I much blame him. That was one crabby ass old man. Despite the fact that momma told me not to contact them again I took a chance and did anyway. I had to find out if daddy was ok. I was glad to hear that it was just chest pains and not a heart attack. I don't know what I would have done if something had of happened to him. Even though I'm a heathen I still love my parents.

At this point my luck was running out. Every time I looked up I was having a close call with someone recognizing me. It was all I could do to stay hidden. And when I did venture out I had to switch up my disguises. I dressed as a woman sometimes, and sometimes as a man. I even had fake beards and moustaches, whatever I needed to do to throw them off.

The money from The Doc had run almost completely out. Since eluding the police at my parent's house I drove until I ended up in Florida and finally settled down in the Everglades. Who would have even thought that someone who had their shit together like me would end up living out of a trailer park in the damn swamp? I had officially sunk to an all new low. I got by on public assistance under a fake identity and turned a few tricks along the way to fill the gap.

A bitch thought her ship had come in when I found out The Doc was coming to town to a Dr's convention. I just knew this would be an opportunity to catch up on old times. Plus I thought the nigga was still in love with me and I could get a few dollars out of his ass. Little did I know that he had come up and considered my ass low budget. The nerve of his black bastard dissing me cause he was doing well for himself, I still couldn't get over that shit.

Since his new found wealth he called himself having a new broad on his arm, some little bird name Persha. I ain't gon' lie she did look better than me since I hadn't been able to keep myself up. But y'all already know how I deal with anyone that gets in my way. I had to let that bitch know that Pebbles was in town. Instead of falling back she tried to jump bold and I had to break her ass off something. As luck would have it I didn't finish the bitch off and she filed a police report. Once they got my description it put them hot on my trail in Florida. My ass has been hiding so deep in the bush you would have thought I was a damn gator.

I did manage to hit a lick and steal some shit from their room before I fled. And that held me over for a little while. I know I should feel guilty about the way I appeared and shook up his world but I didn't. The Doc knew he was playing with fire by telling me that he loved me and was in my corner then switching that shit up just because he had a new bitch, served him right.

I had already been fucked over by one man in my life and I wasn't going out like that again. I had sacrificed everything to love Adrian and to get him to love me only for him to turn on me like rabid dog. In the end I had to put him down but it still ate away at my sanity on a daily basis. I loved Adrian with all my heart and nothing would ever change that. All I could do now was lay low until the heat was down enough for me to make my next move which would land me in Georgia.

Dark Days

As Adrian lay staring at the ceiling he couldn't help but wonder where his life went wrong. How could he have let that nutcase slip by him without noticing any signs? Not only had he been married to a man, he had been having sex with one the whole time. They very thought of his beloved Pebbles actually being Peyton made him sick to the stomach. The time that they were together played out in his mind like a sick and twisted nightmare that he could never manage to escape, even when he was awake.

He had dedicated his life to hunting down Tasha's killer; little did he know she was sleeping in the same bed with him.

He sat up on the side of the bed and wept so hard that his chest actually hurt. His heart bled not only for his son, but for the woman that he thought he married. In the end it was all a lie. That bastard Peyton looked in his face every day like it was nothing. All the while knowing he had woven a web of deceit. Not only was he a killer; he had left Adrian for dead, taking off with the only thing he had left in this world that he loved besides his parents, his son AJ.

To make matters worse everyone knew Pebbles was a man and a killer. There was no way he could go back to work. All of his friends and colleagues knew what had happened. To say that he was embarrassed was an understatement.

He had all but given up hope searching for his son. It was like Pebbles had vanished off the face of the earth. Every lead he and the police had turned into a dead end. There was nothing left to be found of her but bloodstained memories. And even though he was under police protection he lived in constant fear that she might realize he was still alive and try to return and finish him off.

Each attempt made by Adrian to get his life together was met with severe anxiety. Not only did he suffer from posttraumatic stress syndrome, he still hadn't regained full use of his right eye and he walked with a limp. As of late he spent his days indoors with the blinds completely shut. He had also adopted a serious alcohol addiction. He lived on a diet of frozen pizza, top ramen, and malt liquor. The extra twenty pounds he'd gained along with his unkempt facial hair added to his scruffy appearance. His life had changed drastically for the worse. At one point the only thing that kept him hanging on where the memories of his son and saving him from that maniac Peyton.

His only mission in life was finding him and killing him with his bare hands. But what would that then make him? He would be no better than Peyton himself if he had his blood on his hands. Not to mention the fact that murdering someone didn't come as easy for him. And how would his son view him knowing that he killed his mother? Pebbles might not have been AJ's real mother but she was the only one he had ever known.

His emotions teetered between hopelessness, humiliation, and rage. Up until now the latter proved to be the strongest. However these days depression had crept its way into his world and wasn't leaving anytime soon. Against his parents' wishes he turned down every offer for counseling, instead, opting for self-medicating with alcohol. They tried their best to drag him to church, include him on family outings but nothing piqued his interest. Not only would he block their calls, he would leave them knocking outside if they attempted to visit without warning.

He had spiraled into a black hole of despair and couldn't figure out how to pull himself out. Despite the encouragement and support from his family and friends he felt completely alone.

His hands trembled as he picked up the Vicodin bottle and rolled it between his fingers. It was a newly filled prescription and it was time to take a dose. Except this time he wanted to take the pain away forever.

Adrian knew in his heart that his loved ones would be crushed if he did anything stupid but as far as he was concerned his future looked bleak. No one could possibly understand the pain he was in.

He stood from the bed and walked into the bathroom. The overhead light seemed almost blinding to his eyes that become accustom to living in almost darkness. At this point he was sobbing as he stared at his reflection in the mirror. Everything he had worked for and ever loved had been ripped from him. There wasn't any reason to go on. There was nothing else to live for.

He filled up a glass with water before pouring the contents of the entire bottle of pills in his hand.

Adrian had come face to face with his mortality. It was nothing like in the movies. There was no dramatic music. There were no flashbacks over his life, goodbye letter, no voice in his head telling him not to do it. The only noise he could hear was the beating of his heart that was soon about to end.

When it was all said and done he swallowed sixty Vicodin, climbed back into the bed and waited to drift off.

A Mother's Love

"Come on lil nigga, you betta' eat this
shit," I groaned as I attempted to stick a
spoonful of eggs and grits in AJ's mouth.
"Food is getting scarce, plus I gotta get us a
room for a few more months till I can hustle
up on us an apartment." Not only was my baby
cranky and not eating, he was also running a
fever.

I had been on the run now for almost a
year. Not only was my body wearing down
from the mental and physical stress of hiding
out with an infant, the money I had borrowed
from The Doc had run out. I knew it was only
going to be a matter of time before the feds
tracked me down in Florida so I had to uproot
once again. Aside from paying for rooms by
the week, there was gas, food and car repairs.
Not to mention the fact that little AJ was
starting to walk and he hadn't seen a doctor
since I fled town.

I knew had been taking a chance with my baby's health by not taking him to the doctor for regular checkups his first year of life but what was I gonna do? I mean I couldn't risk taking him in for an appointment and having my cover blown. If I went to jail my son would have no one to raise him. At this point part of me wished I had left him with my parents. But I'm not a type of bitch to abandon her child. I don't give a fuck if all I have is a sleeping bag and a crust of bread; he will share them with me. I take care of my own. After all, if I didn't at least have AJ what would all of this have been for have been for?

I decided to suck that shit up and take my baby to the doctor, I would be lying if I said a bitch wasn't scared but I had to do what I needed to do for my baby's health before he got any worse.

Later that day

My hands trembled as I filled out the

registration forms at the nurses station. Not only was I giving false information, I was also using fake identification. I could only hope and pray that my ass wasn't recognized.

After finding a seat in the crowded waiting room I got AJ situated in his carrier and tried to soothe him. My baby was burning up with fever.

"What's his name?" asked another woman who sat across from me in the waiting room. She was a black chick who appeared to be around twenty something years old.

"AJ," I replied. *I hope this bitch ain't about to start getting nosey,* I thought.

"Aww, poor baby he looks miserable. Does he have a cold?" the woman asked.

Bitch, if I knew the answer to that question we wouldn't be here,

"I'm not sure, I'm hoping that's all it is," I answered this hoe hoping she would leave me the fuck alone.

"How old is he?" she asked. "My baby is almost two years old," she announced, turning the baby on her lap so I could see him.

Why is she showing me this little primate?

"Aww, that's a baby... that's for sure." *I ain't about to lie and say this bitch's baby is cute when it's not.*

"Miss Contessa Sanchez," the nurse called out.

I jumped my ass up with the quickness. Her timing was perfect. I needed to get away from this chickenhead asking a million and one questions. Say what you want about my alias, I know I'm not Spanish but my ass do love a good taco and a margarita. I flung my 32 inch curly lace front over my shoulder and hot tailed it into the office.

Little AJ's appointment went off without a hitch. As a mother I was so glad to hear that all he had was a mild upper respiratory infection. The doctor was nice enough to not only give us a prescription for his medication; but some free samples as well. These would definitely come in handy seeing as not only was I running low on cash; it would save me a trip to the pharmacy. The less public appearances I had to make, the better.

Just as I was leaving out of the office two middle aged white women approach me. Judging by the cheap polyester suits they wore and the sternness in their faces they obviously were from some kind of agency and meant business.

"Miss Sanchez may we have a word with you please?"

Oh shit! I wonder what these bitches want.

"A word? For what?" I snapped. I had the sinking feeling that nothing good was about to come of this.

"We just have a few questions for you," one of the women replied.

"What kind of damn questions?"

"Please Miss Sanchez, if you would just follow us, this won't take long at all."

I immediately smelled a rat. Why were they being so damn secretive? And why the hell were they trying to pull me into another room? My first instinct was to clock the one closest to me. If I came across her jaw with a good right hook I might stand a chance at working my way up out of here. My heart raced a mile a minute and it was all I could to keep a straight face without looking nervous. I gripped AJ's carrier tighter in my hand, as it was becoming slippery from my sweaty palms. I decided that the best thing for me to do at the moment was to play it cool. Who knows I may be able to talk my way out of this shit.

That couldn't have been the furthest thing from the truth.

Little to my knowledge the staff was on to me. Come to find out all the hospitals and doctors' offices had been put on high alert since I had fled. There was a nationwide warrant out for my immediate arrest. They were told to look out for a woman or man that fit my description, especially if the person was with a baby. There was a heightened alert not only because I had killed three people; but because I was considered armed and dangerous. I was also wanted for kidnap and child endangerment. It was sad to say, but if I ever had a run in with the police my baby would be the only thing to keep them from shooting me on contact.

I reluctantly followed the two women into the nearby office, all the while my spidey senses were tingling.

"What's so damn important that you felt the need to me to talk to me while I'm trying to get my sick child home? And who are you anyway?"

"Miss Sanchez my name is Skylar Smith and this is Linda Blackney, we are from the department of Child Protective Services we would just like to clear up a few things with you."

I thought I was going to piss on myself at that very moment. These bitches we're trying to hem a sista' up. These heffa were acting all fidgety and shit, like they were waiting on someone. I also noticed that when we entered the room they didn't close the door behind us. If they were truly on to me I'm guessing that they didn't want to be locked up in the room with my crazy ass in case the shit went left. If you ask me, this was wise move on their part.

At this point the only thing on my mind was getting the fuck out of there with my baby. My eyes darted around the room in search of an escape. I noticed that the security guard that was in the lobby was now standing outside of the room with one hand on his nightstick, and a walkie talkie in his other.

Shit just got real, I thought. *Who the hell is he talking to? And why was Child Protective Service fucking with me? They bout' to try and*

*take my baby away from me before the police
get here. I didn't dare sit his carrier down.
They would have to pry him out of my cold
dead hand. I would never let them take my
baby, not as long as I had breath in my body.*

"So yeah what is it that you needed to
clear up? I asked sarcastically, all the while I
was scared shitless. Was this how it was going
to end? I had come too far and had gotten
away for too long, there was no way I was
going out like this.

"Miss Sanchez," Miss Blackney replied.
"May we see your identification please?"

"I showed my ID at the front desk when I
checked in. What's this all about? You don't
have anything better to do then to mess with
minorities?"

I wasn't about to show they ass shit. I just
needed to stall for some time until I figured out
how I was going to make a run for it. That
black ass rent a cop was blocking the doorway,

but the heat was on, and little did he know, his fat ass was about to go down.

"Yes Miss Sanchez we understand that you showed your ID but we need to see it again. There's been a report of a child missing and you fit the description of the abductor."

I know this shit ain't protocol, these dumb broads don't know who they're dealing with. I'm just waiting for one of them to try and play Wonder Woman, they gon' meet this swift left hook.

"I'm appalled! How dare you call me in here for some bullshit like this! As soon as I leave here I'm contacting my attorney!" I barked as I made my way towards the door." Fuck this shit, I'm outta' here."

"Miss Sanchez wait!" one of them called out.

"Now hold on just a second," the guard started, but I cut him off.

"Get the fuck out my way!" I yelled as I slammed him into the wall and stormed passed him. I could hear him yelling on the walkie talkie, "She's headed up front! Call the police!"

"I'm trying!" the receptionist replied." I told you we should have called them as soon as she checked in."

"We had to be sure it was her!" he replied.

This was the trick that dropped the dime on me. I knew it was only going to be a split second before the pigs arrived. Despite the rent a cop talking shit his punk ass had sense enough to fall back. After I made my way back to the lobby I stood directly in front of the receptionist desk and stared that bitch down. I dared her ass to try and restrain me. That heffa was so terrified that she dropped the phone and jumped out of her seat. Ahhh but the bitch wasn't fast enough to get away from me. I reached over the desk and slap that hoe so hard that I knocked her wig sideways. "Next time yo' ass better think twice before crossing Pebbles!" I snapped, before making my way through the lobby and out the front door, leaving everyone in the waiting room stunned.

In a flash I flung the car door open. There was no time to strap AJ in. I tossed his carrier on the floor of the back seat.

"You'll be alright down there boo. You shouldn't get too knocked around."

With that I jumped into the driver's seat and peeled out. These bastards were never going to take me alive!

My Will Be Done

Adrian's body jerked and convulsed before he began to violently puke up blood. He instinctively sat up to avoid choking. Next came a wave of excruciating stomach pains. His body thrashed about on the bed before he finally fell to the floor. His suicide attempt was going nothing like he expected. He planned on fading out peacefully in his sleep. The amount of the drug he consumed was not only enough to stop his breathing and his heart; but shut down his liver and kidneys as well. Little did he know that despite the agony he was in at the moment the vomiting was one of the things that helped to save his life. He was prepared to die that day but apparently God had other plans.

His next blessing would come in the form of one of the church elders that his mother had sent over to check on him. Deacon Andrew came bearing a hot meal and words of encouragement. He was just about to knock on the side door when he heard all the commotion inside from Adrian vomiting and knocking stuff off the dresser as he tried to stand to his feet.

"Adrian! Son, are you ok in there?" he called out.

When he didn't get a response he walked around the house and peeked into Adrian's bedroom window just in time to see him pass out. He called for an ambulance and his mother before kicking the door in.

Once at the hospital his stomach is quickly pumped and an antidote to the drug is administered.

Meanwhile in the waiting room his parents form a prayer circle with some of the other church members. His father who was normally the strong one broke down. He and his wife had already lost Tasha and this was too much for him to bear. His mother screamed out to the Lord and begged him to let her son live. And by his grace their prayers were answered.

When Adrian finally came around he is surrounded by his parents, aunts and a few church members. They were laying hands on him and praying for his well-being.

After a short visit the doctor ordered everyone to leave except immediate family.

"Why didn't you call us before it came to this son?" his father asked through a veil of tears.

Adrian couldn't respond. He could only lay silent as the tears streamed down his own face.

"It's ok baby, we gon' get through this," his mother chimed in. "The Lord spared you for a reason. It's not yet your time. You have family that loves you and needs you, your son needs you. He's still out there Adrian and he needs you to find him."

When it was all said and done he had been broken but not defeated. Through the strength, love and support of his family as well as his faith in God he emerged from the ordeal a stronger man. Before he was allowed to leave the hospital he was required undergo numerous psychiatric evaluations, as well as being under surveillance for any other attempts he might take on his life. He finally committed himself to ongoing counseling which helped him tremendously. In the end his spirit and health were renewed. And he re commited himself to his search for Pebbles for the rest of his life.

Escape The Past

"Dorian, wake up," Mya whispered as she shook her husband. This was the third time this week he'd yelled out in his sleep.

Dorian twisted and turned, clenching the covers before the sound of Mya's voice awakened him from his nightmare. He sat straight up in the bed, trembling, in a cold sweat.

"Baby are you alright?" She asked.

"I'm fine," he replied but his visibly shaken appearance told otherwise.

"I told you my sister's Dr. said he has an opening on Friday. Let's at least stop in and see what he has to say," she pleaded.

"No! I told you I'm ok," he hissed as he jumped up and headed for the bathroom.

These damn dreams had to stop. He had gotten a total of about fifteen hours of sleep in the past four days.

He had finally found the strength to move on with his life since Fallyn's death. She had been brutally murdered by Pebbles and he had the misfortune of having to view her body.

Even though he'd been warned before he entered the room, nothing could have prepared him for what he witnessed. Her flesh had been burned to the bone with acid and her face mangled like she had been thrown to a pack of wolves. Not only had Pebbles scalped her, she'd cut her lips completely off of her face. It had been six years since his phone rang with the news that would change his life forever.

Dorian wiped his face off with a cool rag before heading to the kitchen. Just as he was pouring himself a cold glass of lemonade Mya popped in the room to continue her rant.

"You didn't have to get up," he grunted.

"I'm not going back to bed until I talk some sense into you. You can't keep running from your problems. Something is bothering you and it's not going to go away until you deal with it," she replied.

Mya loved Dorian with all of her heart but one of the things that drove her nuts was his stubbornness.

"I'm not running from anything, I told you I'm just under a lot of stress." It was 2:00 in the morning and here she was trying to argue about a damn dream.

"Dorian who do you think you're fooling? These nightmares have been recurring since we've been married, and who knows how long before that. And you refuse to do anything about them. You can't keep going on like this, they're robbing you of your sleep, and you're becoming crankier by the minute," she responded.

I'm becoming crankier because your ass won't leave me alone about the shit, he thought.

"Look Mya, if it will make you feel any better I'll go to the doctor on Friday. We can call him later today to set up an appointment."

Dorian had no intentions of going to see anyone he just needed to get Mya out of his hair at the moment. He knew that if he didn't at least pretend like he was going along with her idea she would never go back to bed.

"We'll see," she snapped. She'd heard it all before, but it wasn't worth arguing over in the middle of the night. Besides, she didn't want to wake their two year old baby girl, Aniyah.

Once Mya was gone Dorian sat alone at the kitchen table and stared into space. She was actually right; he did need to talk to someone, but what the hell was he going to say? That his ex-crush witnessed a murder and then tried to blackmail the murderer and got murked her damn self? Despite the fact that Fallyn had slipped him into the friend zone, he was crazy about her. It was bad enough finding out that the woman he loved wanted Adrian, but to see her get killed in the process of a dumb ass scheme was too much for him to handle.

He and Mya had been together four years, and married for three. Once he was cleared as a suspect in Fallyn's murder. He immediately moved and changed his phone number. He could still hear the sound of Pebbles' voice when she called him that night. The fact that she was yet to be captured, along with the horrible vision of Fallyn's corpse etched into his memory cause him to lose sleep many nights. Unfortunately he hadn't told Mya any of this. She had never even heard him speak of Fallyn or Pebbles and it was best he kept it that way.

This Little Piggy

Damn this food is delicious, I thought. It seemed like forever since I had a home cooked meal, especially one this good. If I didn't know any better I would have thought my own momma cooked it. The plate consisted of smothered chicken and gravy, homemade mac and cheese, candied yams, turnip greens, and cornbread, complimented with an ice cold glass of fresh lemonade to wash it all down. Even little AJ was eating so fast that he almost choked. I chilled in the kitchen and chowed down on the delicious meal while the couple debated on whether or not they were going to let us stay.

"I say we help her out. You see the chile needs help, plus she got that baby with her. We can't just let the streets have her."

"You don't know a damn thing about that woman Minnie. We barely getting by ourselves and here you want to take in two more mouths to feed," her husband Willie complained.

Minnie pleaded with her husband to let me and AJ stay with them. I could overhear them talking in the next room and from the sounds of it the old man wasn't buying it.

Willie and Minnie Henderson lived and worked on the farm that Willie's family owned since the 1920's, when black folks owned about 14 percent of the farmland in the United States. Since then segregationists, discrimination, poverty and debt accumulation had all of wiped out the existence of the black farmer.

The couple, both grandchildren of share croppers married in 1968 and chose to hold in to the land that held the legacy of his grandparent's dream of being business owners. As of now the black farm owners owned about one percent of the framed land in the US and that number was dwindling swiftly. Even still the Hendersons pressed on with a way of life that many would find menial. Since all of their 8 children had left the land without even a thought of looking back except for rare visits, life had become quite lonely for the elderly couple, especially Ms. Minnie Aside from the neighbors and the few workers that had been around for years, it was just the two of them. Willie suspected that was why his wife was practically begging for him to reconsider me staying with them for a while.

I had held out for as long as I could in Florida but that Everglades shit had gotten old. Not only did my black ass stick out like a sore thumb; the humidity and the bugs were horrid. Not to mention the fact that they were combing the state like crazy looking for my ass after the run in I had with Persha. I lived from pillar to post for the next few years until I finally settled in Georgia.

When I ran into the Henderson's I was actually outside of a general store in a rural area trying to hustle up on enough cash to get a hotel for AJ and I for a few days. That raggedy assed car of mine had long broke down and it now served as our home.

Hiding from the law had taken its toll on me. And having a child go along for the ride only increased the stress. Not only did I want better living conditions for my son and I, AJ was now six years old and beginning to ask more and more questions. I gathered books from the library and tried to homeschool him the best I could but the bottom line was I needed some stability in my life. The last thing a prissy bitch like me wanted was to live on a damn farm, but if I can make it in the damn swamp, I can make it anywhere. Plus if they didn't take us in I didn't know how much longer I could live in these streets.

"You must have forgotten that someone helped us out when we were young. Everybody falls on hard times Willie, you of all people should know that. Besides, I think she will be good company for me at the house."

"I knew it! That's what this is all about? You trying to make a friend?" Willie asked.

"No, it's about doing what's right and helping a woman with a child who can't help herself."

"Bullshit, that's what they have shelters for. I'll be dammed if I let a complete stranger up in here just because you want a buddy. I ain't doing it Minnie so let's just drop it," the 73 year old protested.

Minnie knew that her husband was as crabby and set in his ways as they came, but she also knew that his bark was worse than his bite. It wasn't going to kill them to extend a helping hand.

"They don't have to stay in here with us. The shack in the back has plenty of room for the both of them. It's only temporary until she gets on her feet. She said she was looking for work every day. And I know that baby boy can't eat much."

"Damn woman, you campaigning for her ass like she's family," he vented. "I guess she can stay," he grunted reluctantly.

Yes! I thought *this was just the break I needed. Thank God for Minnie and her kind heart. Cause Lawd knows that ole geezer wouldn't have given me a second look.*

"Now that's the Willie I know," Minnie grinned.

"Now don't go getting ya' hopes up," he replied. "Like you said, it's only temporary. I'll fire up that steam heater in the shack and they will be plenty warm. She and the boy will have to work to earn their keep. She looks like a man, I hope she can work like one," the old man chuckled.

Fuck you pappy! I know a bitch ain't had her hormones in a while but my fine ass was far from looking like a man. I could already see from the jump our asses were going to clash.

"Hush yo' mouth fo' that chile hears you!" Minnie protested, "She's right in the kitchen."

"I don't care if she does hear me; I'm serious as a damn heart attack. She looking like Michael Strahen 'round 'bout the shoulders, back wider than mine. Imma put her big ass on that plow and see what she can do."

I was so happy when he said that we could stay that I let all the cracks about my back fly right out the window. My ass was tired of running and I had finally found a place I could call home.

A few months later

"Momma why we have to work on a farm"" AJ asked as he threw feed to the chickens surrounding his feet. The six year old was starting to look just like his daddy and asking a ton of questions.

"Because we have to work to live here," I replied. "Remember I told you that when we moved in?"

"But I don't want to live here," he whined. "I wanna move back where we were. I want to play with my friends. And I'm just a kid, why do I have to work?"

"You wanna eat don't you?" I didn't mean to snap at him but he was working my last nerve with all these questions. Hell I didn't want to be here anymore than he did.

"Yes ma'am…."

"Look baby, I know you are tired of moving around, so am I. But at the moment we can't do any better. It's either this or living out of the car. It's only going to be for a short while. Things will get better, you'll see."

I was lying through my teeth. The truth was, I had no idea if things were going to get any better. I could only hope for the best. In the meantime I had to keep encouraging my son. He was smart as a whistle and I couldn't just tell him anything.

"Why don't you take a break lil' fella?" Minnie announced from the screen door. "Go wash your hands, there's some cookies and lemonade waiting in the family room for you." She smiled at him as he shot past her to get cleaned up, she didn't have to tell him twice.

"You spoiling him Ms. Minnie," I announced.

"He'll be alright. We still have a few hours till supper. Besides, I miss having a child around here to spoil. Now you come on in here with me and help me with dinner."

"I'm on my way," I laughed. Not only was I tired of these funky ass chickens plucking at my feet. This sun was killing me beaming down on my head. As much as I hate to admit it I kinda liked Ms. Minnie taking such good care of AJ. It kinda made up for the fact that he didn't get to spend time with his real grandparents. She was like his second grandmother.

After I washed my hands she put me on bread duty. I had never kneaded dough a day in my life but according to Ms. Minnie every woman should know how to bake a basic loaf of bread for her family.

As I squished the gooey dough through my fingers I gazed out of the kitchen window across the lush green landscape and thought about how nice it was to finally be able to live in peace. Yeah, true enough we were living in a shack but the land was beautiful even though the work was hard.

"Hold on baby," Ms. Minnie exclaimed. "You have to be gentle with the dough or you are going to make the bread tough."

Now this was the type of shit that annoyed me. I was trying my best and she still had something to complain about.

"I'm sorry Ms. Minnie; I'm trying to be gentle."

"I can't tell, not the way you man handling that dough. And why are your hands so big?"

This bitch thinks just because she's old she can say whatever crosses her mind.
I was all set to cuss her out but I had to go along to get along. I needed a place to lay my head so I had to chill for now.

The next few weeks were the worst. It seemed like the harder I toiled in the hot sun the more chores that old asshole Willie found for me to do. He had the nerve to have my sexy ass working a plow. I did everything from baling hay to slopping pigs. He wasn't lying when he said he was going to work my ass like man. Well I had made up my mind; today I was taking a break. As usual Ms. Minnie had AJ at the main house letting him stuff his face. I was going to take this opportunity to sleep in and relax the rest of the day.

I had just dozed off when I heard knocking at the door. I looked out the peep hole. *It was that damn Willie! I should have known when I didn't show up for duty at the crack of dawn he would have something to say. This bastard might as well be running a boot camp.*

"Yes Willie, what is it?" I know he could hear the attitude in my voice but I didn't give a fuck. Hell I deserved a day off.

"Open the door, we need to talk!" he yelled as he continued to bang.

"I'm resting, what's so important that it can't wait?" I asked, flinging the door open.

"Resting, ain't no time for rest when you live on a farm," he fussed before inviting himself in. If it were one thing Willie couldn't stand it was laziness.

"Willie I'm exhausted, I need to take the day off."

"Now listen here young lady, we had an agreement. You stay here you work to earn your keep. If you can't keep up your end of the bargain then you might need to start looking for somewhere to go."

I could already see where this conversation was headed. Pops wasn't trying to hear shit about me lying around today. I needed to come up with another plan and fast.

All of a sudden it hit me! This muthafucka was old as dirt but he was still a man none the less. I'll just do what I do best; charm him with my feminine wiles. True enough I wasn't the dime I used to be but it shouldn't take much to light a fire in grandpa's pants. Instead of responding I opened my robe and let my lovely lady lumps do the talking.

This outta get his blood pumping, I know Ms. Minnie ain't stack up like this anymore.

"Willie, please can I stay home and relax today? I'm so tired," I cooed as I let my breast fall free from my nightie. "And I was hoping you would keep me company." I batted my eyes at him and blew him a kiss. There wasn't a man alive that stood a chance when I turned on the sex appeal. Before he knew it I had walked up on him and squeezed his little flaccid dick.

"Blech!" Willie turned his head to the side and dry heaved.

"Woman if you don't close up that damn robe... you done made me throw up in my mouth," he ranted in disgust. "And what you grabbing down there for? You ain't gon' come up with nothing but dust."

What an asshole! Now I know damn well my fine ass ain't turning men off like this. He just wants to be a jerk and reject my advances.

"I know I haven't been keeping myself up lately but you just don't know what I've been through," I cried.

I couldn't believe that I had let this fool reduce me to tears.

"I'm sorry I hurt ya' feelings but you caught an old nigga off guard. My shit don't even get hard any more but if it did, it wouldn't be for you, that's for damn sure. And what's goin' on with that Adam's apple? You sure you really a woman?" he asked suspiciously. He squinted his eyes and pushed his glasses up on his nose as he moved in closer to examine my neck I smacked his hand away as he made an attempt to touch my throat.

"Yes I'm a woman! How dare you. Your ass is just so old you wouldn't know beauty if it slapped you in the face. When was the last time you've seen tits this supple and firm? And all you can worry about is my neck?"

Willie moved his glace from my throat down to my chest.

"Lawd you got more chest hair than me." He replied shaking his head in disbelief.

"Fuck you Willie! Just forget it!" I yelled as a wrapped my robe back around my body.

"Look I apologize for making you cry. Imma cut you some slack and let you take the rest of the day off but I expect you to report for duty bright and early."

Thank God! That's all I wanted in the first damn place.

"Thanks Willie, I really appreciate that," I replied as I wiped my nose and eyes.

"It's alright, but don't try to pull a stunt like this again."

"I won't... oh and Willie, can we keep this as our little secret?" I asked.

"Don't worry I won't say nuthin," he chuckled. "Ms. Minnie done been known to whoop a bitch's ass over her man. Don't let the gray hair fool you."

The next day I showed up at the barn bright and early just as Willie expected. I was all set to find out my tasks for the day when he walked up with a pair of what looked like tall rain boots in his hand.

I wonder who he thinks is about to wear those?

"Top of the morning to ya! Imma need for you to put these on," he announced, handing me the boots.

"What are they for?" I asked as I took them from him. I already had a feeling I wasn't going to like what he was about to say.

"They're to protect your feet. We shoveling shit today," he announced as he beckoned towards the horses stable.

"Uhmm excuse me?" This old man was talking like a damn fool if he thought I was going anywhere near shit with a shovel.

"You heard right, we have to get this manure moved onto the truck so it can go out this afternoon for fertilizer. We got a busy day today. After you're done with shit duty you can help clean out the pig's pen. And imma need you to make haste. I don't have time to stand over you and baby sit, I gotta get the rest of these heffas ready for the slaughter house, you understand?" he asked, raising an eyebrow.

"Yes sir I understand," I replied.

I understand that this is my last day working like a damn slave. The fact that he could even prompt his mouth to ask me handle shit was the straw that broke the camel's back. I'm grabbing AJ and we getting the fuck off of this damn plantation!

Goodbye Is Not Forever

"Guess who?" Adrian asked when Dorian answered the phone.

"Who the hell is this?" he asked.

"It's Adrian"

"I don't know any Adrian," he responded, knowing full well he was lying. He knew very well who Adrian was and aside from Pebbles herself this was the last person he wanted to speak to.

"Don't play games man, you know who I am."

Dorian stepped outside on the patio to avoid Mya from hearing the conversation.

"So what if I do? What the fuck do you want and how did you get this number?" he hissed.

"Calm down, no need to get hostile. I don't want any trouble. I just need your help," Adrian replied.

"My help, I don't know anything. I done already had this conversation numerous times with the police. I've moved on with my life and put all this bullshit behind me. So I'm going to ask you nicely, don't ever call me again."

He was just about to hang up the phone when Adrian spoke,

"How you sleeping at night dawg?"

"Man what the fuck you talking about? I told you I don't know shit."

"I'm talking about you helping me catch Pebbles."

Dorian let out a laugh so loud that he had to catch himself and lower his voice.

"You must be smoking crack. If the feds haven't found that crazy muthafucka in all these years what makes you think I can help you? Better yet what makes you think that I want to help you? I have a new life and a beautiful family. I'm not about to put that at risk to help you with some damn witch hunt. Goodbye!"

"Do it for Fallyn."

"Nigga what did you just say?"

"You heard me... don't do it for me, do it for Fallyn."

"Did you hear what I said? I have a family and I've moved on. I don't do the detective thing anymore."

This nigga had truly lost his mind calling me about some bullshit, Dorian thought. *And how the hell did he track me down?*

"Listen man, I know you have moved on but that's all the more reason you should want that monster off the streets. Fallyn's blood is calling out from the grave to be avenged."

At this point Adrian was grasping at traws, trying to say anything he could to get Dorian's help. It had been ten years since the murders had taken place and Pebbles was still at large. Whatever she was doing to elude the police was working. It was apparent that he was going to have to kick his efforts up a notch if he were to ever find his son.

"To hell with Fallyn, she never cared about me," Dorian stated bitterly. "In the end she wanted you."

"Please at least just hear me out. You have your family. I don't have anyone. That's my son out there with that nutcase. I know you don't owe me anything and I'm sorry about the way the shit went with Fallyn, but I know you have got to want this bastard off the streets as bad as I do. What are you gon' do if she tries to contact you? She did it once, she could do it again."

"That ain't gon' never happen. I've moved and changed all my numbers. Pebbles,

Peyton, whoever the fuck he is will never find me."

"I found you….."

As bad as Dorian hated to admit it, Adrian had a point.

"Alright! I'll see what I can do. But this is on MY terms and I'm not making any promises."

Adrian was elated, "thanks so much man! God bless you! You don't know how much this means to me! You can contact me at the number on the caller ID. I have a few leads I want to go over with you when you get the chance."

"Yeah… yeah… I tell you what; you let me contact you, not the other way around. You got that?"

"Aye it's yo' world man! I'll be waiting to hear from you. Thanks again."

It's A Hard Knock Life

It had been a rough ass journey but my baby and I managed somehow to survive. Life of the farm proved too much even for me to handle. When that crazy ass old man thought he was about to have me handling shit I had to raise up. My poor baby and I had to hitch a ride with the damn cows to the slaughter house and from there we kept it pushing till we landed in the Projects of Chicago. As luck would have it, the hood seemed the safest place to hide, go figure.

"Fuck you punk! Yo' momma a crack head!" AJ yelled.

"AJ! Who are you talking to like that?" I yelled as I yanked open the door open to the apartment.

"I'm talking to that punk Mario, he always talking junk. Yeah that's right, you betta' take yo' ass in the house!" AJ blurted out to his friend across the hall.

"Boy get yo' ass in here!"

I tried to snatch a knot in his little ass. "I don't know where you getting that language from but you 'bout to let yo' mouth write a check yo' ass can't cash,"

I don't know what kind of crowd AJ was starting to hang with but his mouth had gotten completely out of control. And since that little nigga turned ten years old he was starting to smell himself. Well I got news for his little ass; I'm the head bitch in charge. The only person cussing up in this house is me.

"I'm sick of him, I'm sick of all those punks making fun of me," AJ fumed as he stomped in the house and threw his backpack on the sofa bed.

I halfway wanted to slap him in his mouth, standing there looking just like his damn daddy. But my baby was having a bad day. And I wouldn't be a good mother if I didn't hear him out and try to encourage him.

"Come sit down son. Listen to me. No matter where you go in life somebody will always have something to say about you. You just have to learn how to have thick skin and tune the haters out."

Now that my child was getting older it was time to start spitting that wisdom to him.

"They not saying anything about me momma, they talking about you." AJ replied, "they saying that you my momma and my daddy."

I knew the years of being on the run had taken its toll on my son. What I didn't know was that he was also feeling the sting of being raised by a single parent. It was time my child learned some hard lessons in life. He was old enough to understand so I had to break it down for him.

"Listen baby, what they are saying is actually true. I am taking care of you like a mother and a father. I know you wish your dad was in your life, so do I, but I'm holding it down for both of us. The reason they talking about us is because the same thing is going on in their household too. Just remember that all that glitters isn't gold. Do you know how many of your friends that are being raised by single mothers? It's a shame but many moms have to take on both roles as father and mother. I mean I'm soft and nurturing when I need to be, I also have to raise you like a man would raise his son, since yo' sorry ass father ain't here. "

I was all set to break the statistics of single parenthood down for his little ass when he said some shit that would shock my world.

"It's not that it at all momma," AJ responded, looking up at me innocently, shaking his head with big fat crocodile tears falling from his eyes. "They not saying you my daddy cause you raising me like a man. They saying it because they say you look like a man."

My head jerked back. I was appalled. Where the hell did these little project bae bae kids get off saying that I looked like a man. I mean I know a bitch done fell off in the past few years, but most of these young bitches out here still couldn't hold a candle to my fine ass.

"A man? They just trying to say something to get under your skin," I replied, trying to play that shit off. But inside I was fuming. "You ain't never heard of playing the dozens? Kids always telling yo' momma jokes."

"It's more than just jokes, they hurt my feelings." he whimpered. "They say you look like a man and you crazy because you don't come out of the house."

"What? That's horrible! Now that's just bullying!"

The part about me not coming out of the house was true. I had to keep a low profile so I only came out when it was necessary to shop or run errands. Other than that a bitch was living like a hermit. I can see where that would look strange, hell it was strange but I had to do what I needed to do to avoid getting caught. Now as far as me looking like a man, imma get to the bottom of that shit.

"That's not the only thing momma," he added.

"What else is it baby?" I asked in concern.

"They make fun of my clothes too," he cried.

I looked over at my son's flooded pants and tight Polo shirt. My child hadn't gotten any new clothes in over a year. I wasn't raised like this and I had my child out here looking like he had been thrown away. It made me feel like a bad momma.

"Get ready son, we going shopping!" I announced.

I'll be dammed if my son gon' be getting teased by these bad assed kids, besides, he deserved it.

"Really? I thought we couldn't afford any new clothes," he asked with a glimmer in his eye.

"Don't worry about that son, didn't I always tell you that I would take care of you? Now you just get ready and let me worry about how much it costs."

"Thank you so much mama," he replied throwing his arms around me. "They won't be able to tease me any more when they see my new clothes," he beamed. "And I don't care what they say, you don't look like a man, you are the most beautiful momma in the world."

"Aww, thank you son," I responded. I could feel a tear forming in the corner of my eye. It was amazing how something that seemed so small could make a child happy.

"You welcome, I love you momma."

"I love you too son."

While AJ got ready I did some prepping. I went into the back of the closet and pulled out my blonde Mary J Blige wig. I made it a point to switch that shit up each time I decided to leave the house. I also wore baggy clothes and slipped on a pair of dark shades.

After we got off the bus and headed into the mall the first place AJ spotted was McDonalds. Leave it to a kid to be hungry as soon as they ass leave the house. I had just fed him a Spam sandwich before we left but he claimed he wasn't full. I didn't have no damn happy meal money. As a matter of fact I didn't have any money except our bus fare back home until my check came next week. But since this was a special occasion I scrounged around in the bottom of my purse and found enough to get him four piece nugget and a small order of fries.

After he got done eating I decided to head over to JCPenny. They had nice school clothes, plus it was always like a mad house in there when a sale was going on. It was just the distraction we needed.

Once we were in the store I headed straight to the boys section and picked out five outfits for AJ to try on, Two in his size and three in the next size up. When he went into the dressing room I followed him.

"Okay baby try these pants on," I said as I handed him the first pair in his size. "Alright, they fit perfect. Now take these other four pair and put them on top of them."

"Don't you want me to take the other ones off?" He asked in confusion.

"Boy what did I say? Put the other pairs on top. And when you're done put the shirts on as well," I demanded, handing him the rest of the clothing.

I peeped my head outside of the dressing room to make sure we hadn't drawn any unwanted attention. Just as I figure it was pure pandemonium; between the mothers running back and forth to bring different sizes to the kids, to the packed isles. It made the perfect backdrop for a getaway.

"But ma why do you have me doing this? Are we about to steal these clothes?"

"Hush your damn mouth and do as I say."

This little nigga was about to get us busted talking all loud and shit. Little ungrateful ass, hell I was doing all of this for him.

"And hurry up," I barked as I yanked a shirt over his head, and then pulled a ski jacket. The winter was about to set in in Chi town and I wanted my baby to be prepared.

"Didn't you say it was wrong to steal?" he asked.

I swear I was about to pop this muthafucka in his mouth, if he said one more word, I'm going to forget that he's my son. This was survival, nothing more, nothing less. And if he was going to make it in this world he'd better 'bout that life if he wanted to continue rolling with me. I mean he was my son and I loved him and all but a bitch had no time for anything slowing her down. You can sit back and judge me all you like, but I done came too far to be sitting up in somebody's jail cell.

"Nigga, if you don't hurry up and put this shit on so we can get out of here I'm going to whoop your ass right here," I snapped.

AJ pouted his lips from me scolding him but he still followed directions. He knew what was up. And if he didn't he was gon' learn today.

"Now when I give you the signal I want you to run your little ass out this store like you was trying out for the Olympics."

"I don't know if I can run that fast with all these clothes on momma."

"Do you need my foot up your ass as motivation?" I asked, giving him a major side eye.

AJ looked down at the floor and shook his head, "No ma'am."

"That's what I thought; now get your little ass ready. And once you get started don't stop for anything, head straight for the exit."

I stepped out first to make sure that there wasn't any plain clothes security. I could spot their asses a mile away.

Once I spotted an open break in the isle I tapped him on his shoulder, "Go!" I yelled as I took off in the direction I wanted him to follow. We knocked several women to the side as we made our way to the store entrance. I glanced back to make sure he was right behind me. As luck would have it his little ass got tripped up and almost fell but he bounced back. Surprisingly no one stopped either one of us. Aside from a few looks from salty customers that we damn near mowed down, we got away Scott free. Still, I couldn't take any chances. Once we got a reasonable distance from the store I dipped into the bathroom in so AJ could catch his breath.

"Momma, I'm tired," he panted as he bent down, placing his hands on his knees.

"Quick in here!" I motioned into a stall. I didn't want to risk standing out in the open in case someone looked in here.

I left AJ in the stall and quickly ran out and pulled off a few paper towels. Once I was back inside I lifted his face up and wiped the sweat from his forehead. This was one of the proudest days of my life.

"You know you did real good back there."

"I'm scared…." he panted.

"Nonsense! I gave you a mission and you handled yourself like a grown man. Yeah, you almost fell but you recovered like true G. That's what I'm talking about."

Hell I never knew when my ass might have to make a run for it and this was good practice for the boy.

"Now gimme these top layers."

I instructed him to quickly remove the first few outfits to allow him to move with a little more ease.

"We got one more stop to make," I announced as I stuffed the clothing in my tote bag.

I figure since luck had been on our side I may as well grab my baby some new shoes as well. Plus I didn't know when I would be able to do this again. I had to strike while the irons were hot.

"Where are we going mama?"

"Footlocker! Lets go!"

Once we arrived at the store I asked the clerk to bring me a pair of the newest Jordan's. I was sending my baby back to school in style.

While she went to go get the shoes I found a secluded corner for us to sit. I nervously watched the entrance anticipating a brigade of police storming the place and taking me down in front of my son. As much as I hated to admit it, this was my worst fear. The whole scenario made me sick to the stomach, not because I was afraid of getting caught, but because I was having damn flashbacks of the last time I was in Footlocker and Peyton showed his ass up. So far I had managed to hide him from AJ when he did appear. That shit would probably scare the daylights out of any child. I don't know what I would tell him.

When the clerk arrived I made sure that the shoes fit, and then I sent her for another pair. Once she was out of sight I instructed AJ to take off with the new shoes on his feet.

He made it out the store but was spotted by a fat assed rent a cop. As soon as he attempted to run after AJ I tripped that bastard. He went down hard, screaming and holding his knee like a little bitch. When he tried to grab his walkie talkie I kicked that shit out of his hand and stomped that shit till it broke into pieces.

"Help! Stop them?" the guard yelled as he attempted to get up.

There were bystanders starting to gawk but as usual in the hood no one said a word. As a matter of fact they were actually cracking up. I figured I better make hast before one of these fools pulled out a cellphone and started recording. The last thing I needed was my ass showing up on World Star Ship Hip Hop. By the time he finally recovered and got ahold of mall security AJ and I were long gone. My baby had not only made it out of the mall, but to the bus stop just as planned. He was already waiting when I got there and we were able to hop on the next bus without any issues.

I couldn't do anything but sit back and smile. It felt good to do a little shopping for my child. Yeah I know, I might not have gone about it the traditional way but my son got what he needed none the less. And he also learned valuable tools that would carry him throughout life that would help him survive. Today it was clothes, who knows, one day it may be food or shelter.

I could tell that AJ was worn out from all the excitement. But it was all going to be worth it when he stunted on them bad ass kids at school tomorrow, speaking of which I still needed to find out who in the fuck was spreading rumors about me being a man.

"So baby, you never did tell mama which one of those little punks said that I looked like a man."

"Huh? It was Mario. He always has something smart to say when I leave out of the house," he replied, lifting his head from off my shoulder, half asleep.

Oh so it's Mario's little ass, I thought. *No wonder AJ was cussing him out. It's about time I taught his little ass a lesson in respect.*

When we finally got off the bus and made it back to the projects I noticed Mario playing outside by himself. I unlocked the door and sent AJ in the house.

"Go on up and put your stuff away. I'll be there in a second."

Here this little motherfucker was looking like a damn Hobbit and had the nerve to say I look like a man, I thought as I made my way over to his bike.

It was the perfect setting, not only was it almost dark outside, no one was watching him.

"What's Up Mario?" I asked. I was two seconds away from snatching his little ass up but I couldn't risk him telling anyone. It didn't matter. The fact that I had caught him off guard cornered him and had him scared shitless was good enough. He looked like he was about to piss on himself.

"Yes ma'am?" He asked nervously.

"I hear you been taking shit. You been telling the other kids that I look like a man?" I asked as I towered over him.

"No.. I..I didn't say that," he stuttered.

"Bullshit! You been fucking with AJ every time he leaves out the house. Well I'm here to tell you that it stops today. You disrespect me and mine imma show you how a man will beat that ass. You got that?"

"Yes..." he replied in a low tone. His voice shook as the tears rolled down his face.

"Good! Now run tell dat!" My voice thundered as Peyton took over and glared down at him.

He stood frozen in fear with his eyeballs damn near popped out of his head. Needless, to say AJ never had to worry about him ever again.

Seven years later

Who's Your Daddy?

"Unless you have some good news for me, don't bother wasting my time," Adrian announced sarcastically after answering the phone for Dorian. He had been waiting for some information from him about AJ for what seemed like an eternity.

"I wish it were that easy to get rid of you," Dorian replied in an equally annoyed tone. "I think I might have some information for you."

"Well, what is it?" Adrian asked.

"I think I might know where your son is. I have a phone number to the school he might be attending."

"What the hell? Are you serious? Hurry up! Give it to me!" Adrian yelled and sat straight up in his seat. These were the words he'd been waiting to hear for almost 18 years.

"Now before you get too excited understand that this may not be the real deal," the detective replied as a bit of caution.

"Man stop bullshittin' and give me the number," Adrian insisted. Even though he had hit a dead end many times over the years looking for his son, it never ceased his excitement each time he got a new lead.

Adrian was beyond ecstatic. Could this be the lead he'd been waiting for?

After receiving the number he quickly hung up the phone. Much to his surprise he was now actually nervous about making the call. What if this was really was his son? What was he going to say to him after all these years? And the bigger question was; if it was really AJ would he even believe him when he told him he was his father?

Who the hell is this? AJ thought as he made his way to the school's office. Someone had called and said that there was an emergency and he was pulled from class. Hopefully nothing had happened to his mom.

"Hello"

"Hello, AJ?"

"Yes this is him, who is this?"

Adrian's heart leaped for joy at hearing his son's voice for the first time since he was a baby.

"It's me son, your father."

"Man yeah right," AJ chuckled. "Quit bullshitting me, who is this for real?" he asked.

"I wouldn't bullshit you son, you just don't know how good it is to finally hear your voice," Adrian responded. It took everything in him to fight back the tears.

At this point the tone in AJ's voice had changed from curiosity to resentment.

"I ain't got no daddy. My daddy walked out on me and my momma when I was a baby." He didn't know who this fool was on the other end of the line but he was about to be introduced to Mr. dial tone very shortly.

"Is that the lie she has been feeding you all these years?" Adrian asked. "I never walked out on you and your momma. You don't know the whole story. I have been searching for you since you were a baby and your mom took you away from me. We need to meet and talk."

By now AJ could feel a lump growing in his throat. If this was really his father he could miss him with all the lies about searching for him. Especially after the way he had treated them. His mother had told him the whole story about how when Adrian found out she was pregnant he demanded for her to have an abortion, claiming that the baby wasn't his. When she refused, he beat her so bad that she almost miscarried.

Pebbles had told AJ that she was young, dumb, and in love. That was the reason she didn't call the police. She told him that she begged Adrian to at least give their relationship a chance for the sake of the baby. As well as the fact that she had nowhere else to turn seeing as her parents were dead. Aside from the brief encounter he had with his grandparents when he was an infant, which he was too young to remember, he had never seen or heard from them so it must have been true. As far as he knew his father stuck around through her pregnancy but had many other women on the side. On the day he was born Pebbles said Adrian came to the hospital and took one look at AJ and said "That little nigga ain't mine."

From that point he told Pebbles that he wanted her out of his house and kicked her out on the street with the newborn baby. Since then they had been living damn near like savages, trying to survive. Not only did AJ hate his father for leaving them He also blamed him for the deep state of depression that his mother was in.

"I don't want to meet you," AJ replied. "You didn't want me when I was a baby, what the hell are you back for now?"

"Son I miss you and I love you. Please let me come and see you and I will explain everything when I get there." Adrian's heart ached over the fact that so much time had been lost. And not only didn't he have the luxury of watching him grow up, that bastard Peyton had poisoned his mind against him.

"Man fuck you!" Adrian spewed. "I didn't need your sorry ass then, and I don't need you now. Don't call me ever again."

"AJ wait!" Adrian yelled. "Don't hang up! Please hear me out! You are in danger. The person that you are living with is not really your mother. His real name is Peyton Edward Jones. He killed your real mother as well as your aunt, my baby sister Tasha."

He knew that he was taking a huge risk by blurting everything out the way that he did but he had no choice. AJ wasn't trying to hear anything he had to say. And he needed to get his attention before he hung up the phone. This was some deep shit that he was laying on him but he had to put something on his mind in case he never heard from him again. Or if he tipped Pebbles off and she fled town before he and the police had the chance to catch up to them.

"Man you crazy as hell," AJ replied before slamming down the phone.

"Is everything all right?" the office secretary asked him. She had been ear hustling the entire time, and she could see also see that his eyes were watery.

"Yeah I'm good."

Just as he was about to exit the office the phone rang again.

"It's for you," she announced after answering the line.

"I don't have anything to say. Tell him I'm not here."

Sensing that she was overstepping her boundaries, the secretary suggested that he take the call anyway based on the fact that it was his father and he said that it was an emergency.

"That's not my father, I don't want to talk to him," AJ pouted.

"If you truly don't think you should talk to him I won't force you, but you may not get another chance," she responded.

AJ sighed, and took the call at an empty desk.

"What do you want? I told you I don't want to talk to you."

"Listen to me son. Please don't hang up; I swear I'm not lying to you. Everything I said about your mother is true. I know that was some pretty harsh stuff to lay on you but I need you to understand what you are dealing with. I'm going to get to you as soon as I can, I promise. Meanwhile don't breathe a word of this to anyone. Take down my number and call me when you get out of school.

AJ pretended to write down the phone number as Adrian called it out. He had no intentions of ever contacting him so there was no need in wasting the ink.

"And whatever you do don't try and confront her. She's very dangerous and I don't want you in harm's way."

"Whatever man...." AJ tried to pretend that Adrian's words didn't have any effect on him when in fact they cut him to the core.

That's What Friends Are For

"If I could jump through this phone and kiss you right now I would," Adrian exclaimed.

Not only had Dorian found his son; against his wife's wishes he agreed to go with him to catch Pebbles and bring AJ home.

"I think thank you will suffice," Dorian replied. "I must be as crazy as you for even agreeing to going along with this crazy shit.

"You ain't crazy, your heart is just in the right place," Adrian responded.

He and Dorian had grown quite close over the years. And the truth was Dorian was actually going along for his own satisfaction as well as helping Adrian out. Adrian knew this but could care less as long as he agreed to help. This would finally be the closure he needed to help him sleep at night. When Mya questioned him about the trip he was about to make, he never gave her any details, instead he told her he was finally going to face the problem that was keeping him up at night. That was all the explanation she needed, for now at least.

Deception

At this point AJ's heart was torn to shreds and he was in a state of confusion. One hand he hated his father for how he had left him and his mother, and on the other he longed for a relationship with him. He cried himself to sleep many nights when he was young; hoping this day would finally come. Despite the awful things his mother had said about his father, part of him still wanted to know him. He didn't know whether he was coming or going. And the bigger question was what if this guy truly was his dad? What if he wasn't? And what if he was really telling the truth about his momma being a shemale killer on the run from the police? For all he knew the guy on the phone could have been a whack job. What other reason would he call him up with such nonsense? It was just all too much to process.

He would skip class later that day and go to the library. There was only one way to find out the truth and that was through doing some research of his own.

The very first thing that he was curious about was the term transgender. He had heard it before but he didn't actually know what it meant. He knew it had something to do with a man dressing up like a woman or vice versa, at least that's what he thought. Once he Googled the term he found out that it was actually a person who are born with typical male or female anatomies but felt as though they've been born into the "wrong body." Many resorted to taking hormones or electing to have sexual reassignment surgery in an effort to change themselves into the opposite sex, thus feeling like they had found they true identity. The very idea of what this meant scared him shitless. Could his mom actually have once been a man?

He made the mistake of hitting Google images and saw operations in progress, as well as genitalia that had been altered to look like the opposite sex. The graphic images grossed him out completely.

"Hey man what you doing in here?" Kenny asked. It was unlike his friend to ditch class and actually go to the library, hell anybody for that matter.

"Huh? Oh I was just getting some studying in," AJ replied nervously. He couldn't hit the escape button to close out the windows fast enough. There was no way he wanted anyone to see what he was looking up out of shame and fear.

"Nigga, since when do you skip class to actually study? I mean where the fuck they do dat at? And what you hiding? You showl closed them damn windows out quick. They won't let us watch porn up in here, so I know that ain't it," he chuckled.

"Well if you must know I'm failing English and I'm trying to squeeze some studying in for this test on Friday." AJ didn't know if this lie was going to be enough to satisfy his friend but he hoped it would so he could get back to the task at hand.

"Look at yo' punk ass acting like a damn mama's boy. Who would have ever thought?" Kenny laughed.

"Fool don't get mad at me 'cause I'm trying to make something of myself."

"True dat, I feel you my nigga. Just hit me up when you get out of this dungeon."

"Bet, I'll hit you up later."

Once the coast was clear AJ resumed his search. The next site he decided to check out would change his life forever as he knew it.

He logged on to the FBI Most Wanted and typed in the name his father gave him: Peyton Edward Jones. His heart sank when he saw a picture his mother on a split screen with another picture of a man that looked exactly like her. The caption read: Peyton Edward Jones aka Pebbles wanted nationwide for murder, attempted murder, child kidnapping, and assault with a deadly weapon, assault with intent to do great bodily harm, impersonating a nurse, eluding the police, identity theft, welfare fraud, and grand larceny.

Despite the evidence that was laid out in front of him AJ remained in denial. This was someone he loved and trusted. The only parent he had ever known. There was no way his loving mother could be this treacherous person. There had to be some kind of mistake. And when he got home he intended on getting to the bottom of it.

Upon entering the house he saw his momma sitting on the couch doing her usual chin maintenance of plucking out hairs. For some reason this never struck him as odd, but today it stood out to him like it never had before. Still, he decided to remain calm and ask few questions.

"Hey baby how was your day? I asked.

"It was alright," AJ replied.

I immediately knew that there was something wrong judging by the tone in his voice and his sullen mannerisms.

"Are you okay son? You look a little down," I asked.

"My father contacted me today," he announced.

I was terror struck! I was so taken aback that I dropped my tweezers and accidentally knocked over my drink.

"I thought he was dead!" I blurted out.

Damn! All these years I thought Adrian was dead and here he was alive. I didn't finish him off after all.....his black ass must have been under police protection all of these years, that's how he managed to slip under the radar.

"Since when?" AJ asked suspiciously.

"Huh? I meant to say he may as well be dead to me," I replied hoping he wouldn't pick up on the lie.

That couldn't have been the furthest thing from the truth. My son peeped that shit with the quickness and immediately shut down. His whole demeanor had changed just that quickly. Still, I had to try and pick him for information.

"So what did he want?" I asked trying not to sound overly eager, when in essence I was mortified. If Adrian was still alive there was no telling how long he had been tracking me. Judging by the fact that he found out where we were and managed to speak to AJ was a little too close for comfort. This meant that the police weren't too far behind. It was definitely time to make another move. But first I had to find out what he knew.

"He didn't want anything…."

"Boy don't play with me! You ran your ass up in here all eager to talk. Don't go mute now. I know he had to want something or else he wouldn't have contacted you!" I yelled.

By now I was in a panic and had stood to my feet. It was apparent that AJ knew more than he was telling. The question was why was he being so secretive? Was he working with Adrian and the police? Don't get me wrong. This was my son and I loved him but if he didn't come clean I was going to have to fuck him up on the spot.

I decided that I could get more flies with honey than vinegar. I planned to make a quick trip to the market to grab something for dinner. I only had a few food stamps left but it was enough to make AJ's favorite meal of smothered pork chops and gravy. I knew for sure I could get him to talk over a good meal.

Skeletons Revealed

AJ moved quickly to pick the lock on his mother's closet door. She was on her way to the market and this was his chance. She had always kept it locked during his entire childhood and he never thought much about it. But since talking to his father and seeing her face on the FBI's most wanted list his curiosity got the best of him. He didn't want to believe all the horrible things that he was exposed too on the internet. Granted he had grown bitter towards her over the years from all the moving around, and the fact that they always seemed to barely be scraping by. For the life of him he couldn't understand why she couldn't get a job like the rest of his friend's moms. It's like she didn't want any better for herself. Whenever he questioned her motives she always broke down in tears and told him that she was suffering from severe depression. At the end of the day he always took her side. After all who was he to question his mother's suffering?

Just as he was about to give up and grab another tool the lock popped open. His heart raced as the door creaked open. Once he was inside he flipped on the light switch. Everything seemed normal on the surface however all it would take was for him to simply move a few clothes and shoes boxes out of the way for the truth to be revealed.

A large black trunk sat against the back wall that had been strategically camouflaged. As luck would have it, it was unlocked. AJ braced himself for what he would find inside. He grabbed the lid and slowly let it fall back. On top were a ton of wigs and bags of hair. Underneath were several sets of men's clothing, including men's shoes. He slowly pulled out each piece for further examination. Next he noticed a rectangle box in a satin bag. Once he slid it out he opened the lid revealing what looked like six dildos in different sizes.

"What the hell?"

Adrian did know want to know that much about his momma if she was using these to play with herself. However as he hurried to put the case back in the bag he noticed that the lid said Velvi Vaginal Dilator.

"This is what they said the men with the fake coochies have to use to keep it open."

He remembered reading up on this during his research. It was becoming blatantly clear that something strange was going on. Maybe it was true after all. Pebbles really had been a man. Before he made his final judgment he decided to dig deeper.

He then pulled out a photo album. The very first picture was of a young boy. He peeled back the sticky paper and removed the photo. The back of it read: Peyton, age 7. He turned the page to see two pictures of the same boy, except this time he was in a photograph with two other children, a girl and a baby boy. When he looked at the back of those they said

Peyton, Bria and Meeko. Were these his siblings?

The next few pages had pictures of the same boy a few years older. In one of the pictures the boy had on girls' clothing.

AJ swallowed the lump in his throat as he fought back the tears. He recognized the boy in the picture as his mother. He sat on the closet floor and flipped through the entire album, revealing the identity of Tasha, his dad's sister and once the best friend of Peyton. They appeared to be around 13 or 14 years of age, and finally one last picture of them that looked to be when they around 18 years of age. Peyton was once again dressed like a female.

AJ cried as he raked through the contents of the chest before pulling out another album. The front of the book was Peyton's entire journey through his sex change documented every step of the way. The tears fell freely as he finally got to the end and saw Pebbles as she was today, as a woman.

So it was true. He was now faced with the reality that the person he thought was his mother was really an imposter and that she had been lying to him his entire life.

"I hate that bitch!" he yelled as he pulled the entire contents of the trunk out onto the floor. "What the fuck else is she hiding?"

When he found the wedding pictures of Pebbles and Adrian he sat on the floor staring at them, trembling and sobbing. This was the first time he got to actually see what his father looked like. The entire time she had told him that he walked out on them when he was a baby. But here sat the photographic evidence of all three of them as a family when AJ was an infant, at the hospital as well as shots of them in the nursery at home.

Upon reaching the very bottom of the trunk he found a secret compartment with a latch. Based on what he had already found out he didn't know if he even had the strength to see what it would reveal. What he would find this time would cause his head to spin. There were hundreds of newspaper clippings that documented the murders of Tasha and his surrogate Fallyn, naming Pebbles as the killer, as well as the murder of Adrian. She told him that he wanted nothing to do with them, when in fact she left him for dead once he found out her true identity. There were also articles from various newspapers discussing the nationwide man hunt for Peyton aka Pebbles.

Everything was true. Pebbles was a sinister killer who had been lying to him his entire life. As he staggered out of the closet his first instinct was to call the police however his shock and disbelief had now turned into pure rage.

His eyes were bloodshot and he gritted his teeth as he made his way to the kitchen to wait for Pebble's to return. It all made sense now. All the running and moving from place to place while he was growing up, never getting the chance to make any real friends, all the stealing, even the occasions that he questioned her about hearing a man's voice coming from her room. It was Peyton the entire time.

It suddenly dawned on him that if she would go as far as killing her best friend and attempting to kill the man she loved, what would make him any different? There was no telling how she would react if she was cornered and felt threatened. AJ decided that it was best that he grab himself a weapon. He pulled the biggest knife from the butchers block, sat at the kitchen table and waited.

Diary Of A Mad Man

When I got back to the apartment I was prepared to throw down on a feast fit for a king. After opening the door I called out to AJ to come grab the bags. The walk from the bus stop had worn me out.

"AJ! Boy do you hear me calling you?" I yelled out for a second time. Much to my surprise he was sitting at the kitchen table with a weird look on his face.

"What's going on?" I panted as I tossed the bags on the counter. "Didn't you hear me calling you?"

"You are a lying bitch and I hate your guts!" he yelled.

Oh shit! What the hell has gotten into this nigga? Did he talk to his father again? I know I wasn't gone that long.

"You done truly lost your fucking mind if you think you can talk to me like that," I yelled. I walked over to AJ with every intention of slapping the taste out of his mouth when he pulled a knife on me.

"You come near me I'll kill you! I know everything! My father was right, you are a man. And you are a murderer. You killed my aunt and that surrogate!" His hands shook and his heart raced as he stared directly in the face of evil. For the first time in his life AJ no longer viewed me as his parent, but as the cold blooded killer that I was.

The blood drained from my face as I listened to my beloved son spew words of hatred. I had been found out and I know it could have only been one person to expose me, Adrian. When I see that son of a bitch again I'm going to pick up where I left off. Meanwhile I had to try and calm AJ down before he did something stupid like call the police.

"Who told you those horrible things about me? Your father? I told you he wants nothing to do with us. I've tried to protect you from him all of your life. Now he's back causing trouble and spreading lies."

"Bullshit! I saw everything with my own two eyes," he ranted as he got up from the table and stormed towards my bedroom.

My eyes immediately focused on the closet door that was open.

"You went through my closet? How dare you invade my privacy!"

AJ ran inside, grabbed two handfuls of the contents of the trunk and threw it in the middle of the floor.

"You are a fucking liar! Here's the proof of everything," he screamed.

Before I knew I had switched to Peyton and grabbed him by his throat, lifting him off the floor.

"Look here you little ungrateful runt, I suggest you learn some fucking manners!" he belted out. "You wouldn't even be here if it wasn't for me!"

AJ's legs dangled as he tried to pry my hands from around his neck. In his haste he had left the knife on the kitchen table. Once Peyton was comfortable that his message was received he dropped AJ, leaving him on the ground holding his neck and gasping for air.

The whole scenario of my baby looking up at me with those big brown eyes tugged at my heart. Before I knew it I had switched back to my normal self.

"I'm sorry baby! Momma didn't mean to hurt you," I cried. My son was looking up at me with sheer terror in his eyes. If it were anyone else I would have been thrilled, but I never wanted my baby to fear me. I went over to try and console him but he scrambled to his feet and pushed me away. I could tell by the way he kept glancing at the bedroom door that he wanted to make an escape but I couldn't let that happen.

"Listen to me sweetheart; I never wanted you to find any of this out. Your father and I were supposed to live happily ever after but he ruined everything. You were the blessing that made the story complete. We were supposed to be one big happy family, but noooo Adrian had to go and fuck everything up," I ranted as I paced the floor.

The memories of all that I had gone through came flooding back like a tidal wave.

"You ruined everything by lying about who you really were!" AJ spewed. "You are a pervert who tricked my father into thinking you were a woman. And you tried to kill him when he found out the truth, just like you butchered those women."

AJ's fear had now resorted back to anger as he stood toe to toe with me, yelling in my face.

"You truly have a death wish, don't you lil' nigga?" Peyton asked.

"Who is that? Peyton, the punk bitch that you started out as before you got your nuts cut. What you gon' do kill me too you sicko?" AJ asked. His nostrils flared and his stance was ready for battle.

"Hush Peyton!" I said to myself.

It was true, I was a sicko. I tried my damndest to control Peyton from coming out, and most of the time I was successful. But each and every time I felt cornered or threatened he reappeared.

Meanwhile with Adrian and Dorian

"Step on it! My son could be in danger at this very moment," Adrian yelled from the passenger seat. He'd offer to drive but Dorian wasn't having it. He was in a state of panic and would have gotten them both killed.

"I'm going as fast as the law will allow," he replied as he mashed down the gas pedal, speeding down the freeway.

"Fuck the law! I'm trying to get to my son before it's too late."

Adrian had the sinking feeling that after he contacted AJ that he would try and confront Pebbles despite his warnings. This would be a fatal mistake on his part. He had no idea who he was dealing with or what she was capable of. . It was bad enough he hadn't been there for him his entire life. He couldn't live with himself if something happened to him behind all of this.

"Man I got this, just sit back and try to relax."

"Ha! That's easier said than done. You sure you have the right address?"

"Yep! We'll be riding down on this asshole in no time. And remember I don't want to be anywhere around when the police arrive," he reminded Adrian.

"Gotcha!"

Peyton, Pebbles, and AJ

"AJ please try and understand that everything I did was out of love for you and your father. I didn't want to hurt those girls, especially your aunt Tasha. I loved her, but they tried to stand in the way of true love."

"Go to hell!" AJ yelled before pushing me out of the way and storming out of the room. He headed straight for the kitchen and grabbed the knife. When he turned to draw it on me I had a trick for his ass. Not only had I switched back to Peyton; I had pulled out the revolver I kept in a secret compartment in the pantry. Yeah I knew it was a bit extreme but I already had my mind made up that if shit went foul like it was at this very moment I wasn't being taken alive. I had gotten away with too much and for too long. If the cops wanted me they would have to take me by force. A bitch like me was going out like Cleo in Set It Off.

Peyton cocked the barrel and pointed it straight at AJ's head.

"Where's all that mouth now muthafucka! Drop that fucking knife and put your hands in the air."

My child started to cry when he saw his life about to come to an end. I didn't want to kill AJ. He was the only thing I had left in this world that meant anything to me. My maternal instincts kicked in and I switched back.

"AJ I love you so much. I did all of this for you, for us. Let's just get out of here and we can put all of this behind us," I pleaded.

"That's where you fucked up with Adrian," Peyton snapped. "Tryin' to reason instead of finishing the fucking job! Kill him and let's get out of here!"

AJ looked on in horror as I argued with myself over taking his life.

"Kiss my ass Peyton! This is my baby boy! I love him."

"Bitch! You standing here arguing with YOURSELF. Face it; you are a fucking whack job. After you finish off this little twerp you may as well take me out of my misery as well," he yelled.

This was a new development, not only did Peyton want me to kill AJ, he wanted me to turn the gun on myself.

While Peyton and I went back and forth AJ took this as his opportunity to make his move. He overpowered me, we tussled and he ended up taking the gun.

"You done fucked up now for real, you simple bitch! You let him get the gun!" Peyton yelled at me.

"Shut up! Both of you!" AJ belted out. The bickering between myself and Peyton was not only working his last nerve; but it served as a terrifying reminder of just how twisted my brain had become.

"Get down on your knees and put your hands where I can see them," AJ sobbed. "You have hurt too many people; I'm not letting you hurt anyone else."

"Son, please. You don't want to do this. I love you." I cried out to him, hoping that he would see me as the mother who had always loved him and had his back.

For a split second my planned worked. AJ's entire body shook with fear and the sweat beaded up on his forehead. He had come face to face with killing the only mother he had ever known. Regardless of who I was, and how much he hated me at the moment there was still a side of him that loved me.

"I love you too momma," he cried.

I could tell that he didn't want to pull the trigger. It was at that very moment as I sat there defeated I had a moment of clarity. My entire life with AJ flashed in front of me. From the first time I held him in my arms as an infant, to his first day of school.

I realized that I was sick in the head to the point of no return. But despite the fact that I loved AJ with all my heart I knew that if he were to let me go free I was going to do what I needed to do to get away. For the past 17 years the child that stood before me with a gun in his hand owned a piece of my heart, and for that he at least deserved a warning.

"AJ I love you baby….. but only one of us is walking out of here alive today. If you let me go I will kill you, so I suggest that you choose wisely."

There was nothing else to be said. Without giving it a second thought AJ pulled the trigger. Splattering half of my face and casing him to jerk back from the impact.

Nightmare Ended

Adrian arrived just in time to hear the gun go off. His heart was in his stomach as he pictured Pebbles killing AJ. He kicked the door in and screamed out for him.

"AJ!! Where are you son?"

His question was answered when he saw AJ standing over Pebbles' body that was surrounded in a pool of blood. AJ dropped the weapon, looked over at his father and they finally embraced for the first time since he was a baby. He couldn't believe that his nightmare had finally come to an end.

Once the police arrived and secured the crime scene the investigation was underway. AJ would eventually get to go free based on his claim of self-defense. He and Adrian would spend the rest of their days making up for lost time and putting the pieces of their life back together.

The End

Midnite Love

If you have enjoyed this series please leave a review. Also be sure to check out my other titles under Midnite Love as well as Lady Onyxx. And as always thank you for the continued support.

53746394R00083

Made in the USA
Lexington, KY
17 July 2016